THE TEETH OF THE TIGER

THE TEETH OF THE TIGER

TOM CLANCY

G. P. PUTNAM'S SONS ◇ NEW YORK

⫿P

G. P. Putnam's Sons
Publishers Since 1838
a member of
Penguin Group (USA) Inc.
375 Hudson Street
New York, NY 10014

Library of Congress Cataloging-in-Publication Data

Clancy, Tom, date.
The teeth of the tiger / Tom Clancy.
p.   cm.
ISBN 0-399-15079-X
ISBN 0-399-15136-2 (Limited edition)
1. Ryan, Jack (Fictitious character)—Fiction.   2. Terrorism—Prevention—Fiction.
3. Children of presidents—Fiction.   4. Intelligence officers—Fiction.
5. Fathers and sons—Fiction.   6. Drug traffic—Fiction.   I. Title.
PS3553.L245T+44   2003   2003047125
813'.54—dc21

Printed in the United States of America
1   3   5   7   9   10   8   6   4   2

This book is printed on acid-free paper. ∞

BOOK DESIGN BY LOVEDOG STUDIO

To Chris and Charlie.
Welcome aboard

. . . and, of course, Lady Alex, whose light burns
as brightly as ever

ACKNOWLEDGMENTS

Marco, in Italy, for navigation instructions
Ric and Mort for the medical education
Mary and Ed for the maps
Madam Jacque for the records
UVA for the look at TJ's place
Roland, again, for Colorado
Mike for the inspiration
And a raft of others for small but important tidbits of knowledge

"People sleep peaceably in their beds at night only because rough men stand ready to do violence on their behalf."

—GEORGE ORWELL

"This is a war of the unknown warriors; but let all strive without failing in faith or in duty . . ."

—WINSTON CHURCHILL

Whether the State can loose and bind
 In Heaven as well as on Earth:
If it be wiser to kill mankind
 Before or after the birth—
These are matters of high concern
 Where State-kept schoolmen are;
But Holy State (we have lived to learn)
 Endeth in Holy War.

Whether The People be led by The Lord,
 Or lured by the loudest throat:
If it be quicker to die by the sword
 Or cheaper to die by vote—
These are things we have dealt with once,
 (And they will not rise from their grave)
For Holy People, however it runs,
 Endeth in wholly Slave.

Whatsoever for any cause,
 Seeketh to take or give
Power above or beyond the Laws,
 Suffer it not to live!
Holy State or Holy King—
 Or Holy People's Will—
Have no truck with the senseless thing.
 Order the guns and kill!
Saying—after—me:—

Once there was The People—Terror gave it birth;
Once there was The People and it made a Hell of Earth
Earth arose and crushed it. Listen, O ye slain!
Once there was The People—it shall never be again!

   —RUDYARD KIPLING, "Macdonough's Song"

THE TEETH OF THE TIGER

THE OTHER SIDE OF THE RIVER

DAVID GREENGOLD had been born in that most American of communities, Brooklyn, but at his Bar Mitzvah, something important had changed in his life. After proclaiming "Today I am a man," he'd gone to the celebration party and met some family members who'd flown in from Israel. His uncle Moses was a very prosperous dealer in diamonds there. David's own father had seven retail jewelry stores, the flagship of which was on Fortieth Street in Manhattan.

While his father and his uncle talked business over California wine, David had ended up with his first cousin, Daniel. His elder by ten years, Daniel had just begun work for the Mossad, Israel's main foreign-intelligence agency, and, a quintessential newbie, he had regaled his cousin with stories. Daniel's obligatory military service had been with the Israeli paratroopers, and he'd made eleven jumps, and had seen some action in the 1967 Six Day War. For him, it had been a happy war, with no serious casualties in his company, and just enough kills to make it seem to have been a sporting adventure—a hunting trip against game that was dangerous, but not overly so, with a conclusion that had fitted very well indeed with his prewar outlook and expectations.

The stories had provided a vivid contrast to the gloomy TV coverage of Vietnam that led off every evening news broadcast then, and with the enthusiasm of his newly reaffirmed religious identity, David had decided on the spot to emigrate to his Jewish homeland as soon as he graduated from high school. His father, who'd served in the U.S. Second Armored Division in the Second World War, and on the whole found the adventure less than pleasing, had been even less happy by the possibility of his son's going to an Asian jungle to fight a war for which neither he nor any of his acquaintances had much enthusiasm—and so, when graduation came, young David flew El Al to Israel and really never looked back. He brushed up on his Hebrew, served his uniformed time, and then, like his cousin, he was recruited by the Mossad.

In this line of work, he'd done well—so well that today he was the Station Chief in Rome, an assignment of no small importance. His cousin Daniel, meanwhile, had left and gone back to the family business, which paid far better than a civil servant's wage. Running the Mossad Station in Rome kept him busy. He had three full-time intelligence officers under his command, and they took in a goodly quantity of information. Some of this information came from an agent they called Hassan. He was Palestinian by ancestry, and had good connections in the PFLP, the Popular Front for the Liberation of Palestine, and the things he learned there he shared with his enemies, for money—enough money, in fact, enough to finance a comfortable flat a kilometer from the Italian parliament building. David was making a pickup today.

The location was one he'd used before, the men's room of the Ristorante Giovanni near the foot of the Spanish Steps. First taking the time to enjoy a lunch of Veal Francese—it was superb here—he finished his white wine and then rose to collect his package. The dead drop was on the underside of the leftmost urinal, a theatrical choice but it had the advantage of never being inspected or cleaned. A steel plate had been glued there, and even had it been noticed, it would have looked innocent enough, since the plate bore the embossed name of the manufacturer, and a number that meant nothing at all. Approaching it, he decided to take advantage of the opportunity by doing what men usually do with a urinal, and, while engaged, he heard the door creak open. Whoever it was took no interest in him, however, but, just to make sure, he dropped his cigarette pack, and as he bent down to retrieve it with his right hand, his left snatched the magnetic package off its hiding place. It was good fieldcraft, just like a professional magician's, attracting attention with the one hand and getting the work done with the other.

Except in this case it didn't work. Scarcely had he made the pickup when someone bumped into him from behind.

"Excuse me, old man—*signore,* that is," the voice corrected itself in what sounded like Oxford English. Just the sort of thing to make a civilized man feel at ease with a situation.

Greengold didn't even respond, just turned to his right to wash his hands and take his leave. He made it to the sink, and turned on the water, when he looked in the mirror.

Most of the time, the brain works faster than the hands. This time he saw the blue eyes of the man who had bumped into him. They were ordinary enough, but their expression was not. By the time his mind had commanded his body to react, the man's left hand had reached forward to grab his forehead, and something cold and sharp bit into the back of his neck, just below the skull. His head was pulled sharply backward, easing the passage of the knife into his spinal cord, severing it completely.

Death did not come instantly. His body collapsed when all of the electrochemical commands to his muscles ceased. Along with that went all feeling. Some distant fiery sensations at his neck were all that remained, and the shock of the moment didn't allow them to grow into serious pain. He tried to breathe, but couldn't comprehend that he would never do that again. The man turned him around like a department store mannequin and carried him to the toilet stall. All he could do now was look and think. He saw the face, but it meant nothing to him. The face looked back, regarding him as a thing, an object, without even the dignity of hatred. Helplessly, David scanned with his eyes as he was set down on the toilet. The man appeared to reach into his coat to steal his wallet. Was that what this was, just a robbery? A robbery of a senior Mossad officer? Not possible. Then the man grabbed David by the hair to lift up his drooping head.

"Salaam aleikum," his killer said: Peace be unto you. So, this was an

Arab? He didn't look the least bit Arabic. The puzzlement must have been evident on his face.

"Did you really trust Hassan, Jew?" the man asked. But he displayed no satisfaction in his voice. The emotionless delivery proclaimed contempt. In his last moments of life, before his brain died from lack of oxygen, David Greengold realized that he'd fallen for the oldest of espionage traps, the False Flag. Hassan had given him information so as to be able to identify him, to draw him out. Such a stupid way to die. There was time left for only one more thought:

Adonai echad.

The killer made sure his hands were clean, and checked his clothing. But knife thrusts like this one didn't cause much in the way of bleeding. He pocketed the wallet, and the dead-drop package, and after adjusting his clothing made his way out. He stopped at his table to leave twenty-three Euros for his own meal, including only a few cents for the tip. But he would not be coming back soon. Finished with Giovanni's, he walked across the square. He'd noticed a Brioni's on his way in, and he felt the need for a new suit.

HEADQUARTERS, United States Marine Corps, is not located in the Pentagon. The largest office building in the world has room for the Army, Navy, and Air Force, but somehow or other the Marines got left out, and have to satisfy themselves with their own building complex called the Navy Annex, a quarter of a mile away on Lee Highway in Arlington, Virginia. It isn't that much of a sacrifice. The Marines have always been something of a stepchild of the American military, technically a subordinate part of the Navy, where their original utility was to be the Navy's private army, thus precluding the need to embark soldiers on warships, since the Army and the Navy were never supposed to be friendly.

Over time, the Marine Corps became a rationale unto itself, for more than a century the only American land fighting force that foreigners ever saw. Absolved of the need to worry about heavy logistics, or even medical personnel—they had the squids to handle that for them—every Marine was a rifleman, and a forbidding, sobering sight to anyone who did not have a warm spot in his heart for the United States of America. For this reason, the Marines are respected, but not always beloved, among their colleagues in America's service. Too much show, too much swagger, and too highly developed a sense of public relations for the more staid services.

The Marine Corps acts like its own little army, of course—it even has its own air force, small, but possessed of sharp fangs—and that now included a chief of intelligence, though some uniformed personnel regarded that as a contradiction in terms. The Marine intelligence headquarters was a new establishment, part of the Green Machine's effort to catch up with the rest of the services. Called the M-2—"2" being the numerical identifier of someone in the information business—the chief's name was Major General Terry Broughton, a short, compact professional infantryman who'd been stuck with this job in order to bring a little reality to the spook trade: the Corps had decided to remember that at the end of the paper trail was a man with a rifle who needed good information in order to stay alive. It was just one more secret of the Corps that the native intelligence of its personnel was second to none—even to the computer wizards of the Air Force whose attitude was that anyone able to fly an airplane just *had to be* smarter than anybody else. Eleven months from now, Broughton was in line to take command of the Second Marine Division, based at Camp Lejeune, North Carolina. This welcome news had just arrived a week before, and he was still in the best of good moods from it.

That was good news for Captain Brian Caruso as well, for whom an audience with a general officer was, if not exactly frightening, certainly reason for a little circumspection. He was wearing his Class-A olive-colored uniform, complete to the Sam Browne belt, and all the ribbons to which he was entitled, which wasn't all that many, though some of them were kind of pretty, as well as his gold parachute-jumper's wings, and a collection of marksmanship awards large enough to impress even a lifelong rifleman like General Broughton.

The M-2 rated a lieutenant-colonel office boy, plus a black female gunnery sergeant as a personal secretary. It all struck the young captain as odd, but nobody had ever accused the Corps of logic, Caruso reminded himself. As they liked to say: two hundred thirty years of tradition untrammeled by progress.

"The General will see you now, Captain," she said, looking up from the phone on her desk.

"Thank you, Gunny," Caruso said, coming to his feet and heading for the door, which the sergeant held open for him.

Broughton was exactly what Caruso had expected. A whisker under six feet, he had the sort of chest that might turn away a high-speed bullet. His hair was a tiny bit more than stubble. As with most Marines, a bad hair day was what happened when it got to half an inch, and required a trip to the barber. The general looked up from his paperwork and looked his visitor up and down with cold hazel eyes.

Caruso did not salute. Like naval officers, Marines do not salute unless under arms or "covered" with a uniform cap. The visual inspection lasted about three seconds, which only felt like a week or so.

"Good morning, sir."

"Have a seat, Captain." The general pointed to a leather-covered chair.

Caruso did sit down, but remained at the position of attention, bent legs and all.

"Know why you're here?" Broughton asked.

"No, sir, they didn't tell me that."

"How do you like Force Recon?"

"I like it just fine, sir," Caruso replied. "I think I have the best NCOs in the whole Corps, and the work keeps me interested."

"You did a nice job in Afghanistan, says here." Broughton held up a folder with red-and-white-striped tape on the edges. That denoted top-secret material. But special-operations work often fell into that category, and, sure as hell, Caruso's Afghanistan job had not been something for the *NBC Nightly News*.

"It was fairly exciting, sir."

"Good work, says here, getting all your men out alive."

"General, that's mostly because of that SEAL corpsman with us. Corporal Ward got shot up pretty bad, but Petty Officer Randall saved his life, and that's for sure. I put him in for a decoration. Hope he gets it."

"He will," Broughton assured him. "And so will you."

"Sir, I just did my job," Caruso protested. "My men did all—"

"And that's the sign of a good young officer," the M-2 cut him off. "I read your account of the action, and I read Gunny Sullivan's, too. He says you did just fine for a young officer in his first combat action." Gunnery Sergeant Joe Sullivan had smelled the smoke before, in Lebanon and Kuwait, and a few other places that had never made the TV news. "Sullivan worked for me once," Broughton informed his guest. "He's due for promotion."

Caruso bobbed his head. "Yes, sir. He's sure enough ready for a step up in the world."

"I've seen your fit-rep on him." The M-2 tapped another folder, this one not with TS formatting. "Your treatment of your men is generous in its praise, Captain. Why?"

That made Caruso blink. "Sir, they did very well. I could not have expected more under any circumstances. I'll take that bunch of Marines up against anybody in the world. Even the new kids can all make sergeant someday, and two of them have 'gunny' written all over them. They work hard, and they're smart enough that they start doing the right thing before I have to tell them. At least one of them is officer material. Sir, those are my people, and I am damned lucky to have them."

"And you trained them up pretty well," Broughton added.

"That's my job, sir."

"Not anymore, Captain."

"Excuse me, sir? I have another fourteen months with the battalion, and my next job hasn't been determined yet." Though he'd happily stay in Second Force Recon forever. Caruso figured he'd screen for major soon, and maybe jump to battalion S-3, operations officer for the division's reconnaissance battalion.

"That Agency guy who went into the mountains with you, how was he to work with?"

"James Hardesty, says he used to be in the Army Special Forces. Age forty or so, but he's pretty fit for an older guy, speaks two of the local languages. Doesn't wet his pants when bad things happen. He—well, he backed me up pretty well."

The TS folder went up again in the M-2's hands. "He says here you saved his bacon in that ambush."

"Sir, nobody looks smart getting into an ambush in the first place. Mr. Hardesty was reconnoitering forward with Corporal Ward while I was getting the satellite radio set up. The bad guys were in a pretty clever little spot, but they tipped their hand. They opened up too soon on Mr. Hardesty, missed him with their first burst, and we maneuvered uphill around them. They didn't have good enough security out. Gunny Sullivan took his squad right, and when he got in position, I took my bunch up the middle. It took a total of ten to fifteen minutes, and then Gunny Sullivan got our target, took him right in the head from ten meters. We wanted to take him alive, but that wasn't possible the way things played out." Caruso shrugged. Superiors could generate officers, but not the exigencies of the moment, and the man had had no intention of spending time in American captivity, and it was hard to put the bag on someone like that. The final score had been one badly shot-up Marine, and sixteen dead Arabs, plus two live captives for the Intel pukes to chat with. It had ended up being more productive than anyone had expected. The Afghans were brave enough, but they weren't madmen—or, more precisely, they chose martyrdom only on their own terms.

"Lessons learned?" Broughton asked.

"There is no such thing as too much training, sir, or being in too good a shape. The real thing is a lot messier than exercises. Like I said, the Afghans are brave enough, but they are not trained. And you can never know which ones are going to slug it out, and which ones are going to cave. They taught us at Quantico that you have to trust your instincts, but they don't issue instincts to you, and you can't always be sure if you're listening to the right voice or not." Caruso shrugged, but he just went ahead and spoke his mind. "I guess it worked out okay for me and my Marines, but I can't really say I know why."

"Don't think too much, Captain. When the shit hits the fan, you don't have time to think it all the way through. You think beforehand. It's in how you train your people, and assign responsibilities to them. You prepare your mind for action, but you never think you know what form the action is going to take. In any case, you did everything pretty well. You impressed this Hardesty guy—and he *is* a fairly serious customer. That's how this happened," Broughton concluded.

"Excuse me, sir?"

"The Agency wants to talk to you," the M-2 announced. "They're doing a talent hunt, and your name came up."

"To do what, sir?"

"Didn't tell me that. They're looking for people who can work in the field. I don't think it's espionage. Probably the paramilitary side of the house. I'd guess that's the new counterterror shop. I can't say I'm pleased to lose a promising young Marine. However, I have no say in the matter. You are free to decline the offer, but you do have to go up and talk to them beforehand."

"I see." He didn't, really.

"Maybe somebody reminded them of another ex-Marine who worked out fairly well up there . . ." Broughton half observed.

"Uncle Jack, you mean? Jesus—excuse me, sir, but I've been dodging that ever since I showed up at the Basic School. I'm just one more Marine O-3, sir. I'm not asking for anything else."

"Good," was all Broughton felt like saying. He saw before him a very promising young officer who'd read the *Marine Corps Officer's Guide* front to back, and hadn't forgotten any of the important parts. If anything he was a touch too earnest, but he'd been the same way once himself. "Well, you're due up there in two hours. Some guy named Pete Alexander, another ex–Special Forces guy. Helped run the Afghanistan operation for the Agency back in the 1980s. Not a bad guy, so I've heard, but he doesn't want to grow his own talent. Watch your wallet, Captain," he said in dismissal.

"Yes, sir," Caruso promised. He came to his feet, into the position of attention.

The M-2 graced his guest with a smile. "Semper Fi, son."

"Aye, aye, sir." Caruso made his way out of the office, nodded to the gunny, never said a word to the half-colonel, who hadn't bothered looking up, and headed downstairs, wondering what the hell he was getting into.

HUNDREDS OF miles away, another man named Caruso was thinking the same thing. The FBI had made its reputation as one of America's premier law-enforcement agencies by investigating interstate kidnappings, beginning soon after passage of the Lindbergh Law in the 1930s. Its success in closing such cases had largely put an end to kidnapping-for-money—at least for smart criminals. The Bureau closed *every single one* of those cases, and professional criminals had finally caught on that this form of crime was a sucker's game. And so it had remained for years, until kidnappers with objectives other than money had decided to delve into it.

And those people were much harder to catch.

Penelope Davidson had vanished on her way to kindergarten that very morning. Her parents had called the local police within an hour after her disappearance, and soon thereafter the local sheriff's office had called the FBI. Procedure allowed the FBI to get involved as soon as it was possible for the victim to have been taken across a state line. Georgetown, Alabama, was just half an hour from the Mississippi state line, and so the Birmingham office of the FBI had immediately jumped on the case like a cat on a mouse. In FBI nomenclature, a kidnapping case is called a "7," and nearly every agent in the office got into his car and headed southwest for the small farming-market town. In the mind of each agent, however, was the dread of a fool's errand. There was a clock on kidnapping cases. Most victims were thought to be sexually exploited and killed within four or six hours. Only a miracle could get the child back alive that quickly, and miracles didn't happen often.

But most of them were men with wives and children themselves, and

so they worked as though there were a chance. The office ASAC—
Assistant Special Agent in Charge—was the first to talk to the local sheriff,
whose name was Paul Turner. The Bureau regarded him as an amateur
in the business of investigations, out of his depth, and Turner thought
so as well. The thought of a raped and murdered little girl in his jurisdiction turned his stomach, and he welcomed federal assistance. Photos
were passed out to every man with a badge and a gun. Maps were con-
sulted. The local cops and FBI Special Agents headed to the area be-
tween the Davidson house and the public school to which she'd walked
five blocks every morning for two months. Everyone who lived on that
pathway was interviewed. Back in Birmingham, computer checks were
made of possible sex offenders living within a hundred-mile radius,
and agents and Alabama state troopers were sent to interview them, too.
Every house was searched, usually with permission of the owner, but
often enough without, because the local judges took a stern view of kidnapping.

For Special Agent Dominic Caruso, it wasn't his first major case, but
it was his first "7," and while he was unmarried and childless, the
thought of a missing child caused his blood first to chill, and then to
boil. Her "official" kindergarten photo showed blue eyes and blond hair
turning brown, and a cute little smile. This "7" wasn't about money. The
family was working class and ordinary. The father was a lineman for
the local electric co-op, the mother worked part-time as a nurse's aide in
the county hospital. Both were churchgoing Methodists, and neither, on
first inspection, seemed a likely suspect for child abuse, though that
would be looked into, too. A senior agent from the Birmingham Field
Office was skilled in profiling, and his initial read was frightening: this
unknown subject could be a serial kidnapper and killer, someone who
found children sexually attractive, and who knew that the safest way to
commit this crime was to kill the victim afterward.

He was out there somewhere, Caruso knew. Dominic Caruso was a
young agent, hardly a year out of Quantico, but already in his second
field assignment—unmarried FBI agents had no more choice in picking
their assignments than a sparrow in a hurricane. His initial assignment
had been in Newark, New Jersey, all of seven months, but Alabama was

more to his taste. The weather was often miserable, but it wasn't a bee-hive like that dirty city. His assignment now was to patrol the area west of Georgetown, to scan and wait for some hard bit of information. He wasn't experienced enough to be an effective interviewer. The skill took years to develop, though Caruso thought he was pretty smart, and his college degree was in psychology.

Look for a car with a little girl in it, he told himself, *one* not *in a car seat?* he wondered. It might give her a better way to look out of the car, and maybe wave for help . . . So, no, the subject would probably have her tied up, cuffed, or wrapped with duct tape, and probably gagged. *Some little girl, helpless and terrified.* The thought made his hands tighten on the wheel. The radio crackled.

"Birmingham Base to all '7' units. We have a report that the '7' suspect might be driving a white utility van, probably a Ford, white in color, a little dirty. Alabama tags. If you see a vehicle matching that description, call it in, and we'll get the local PD to check it out."

Which meant, don't flash your gum-ball light and pull him over yourself unless you have to, Caruso thought. It was time to do some thinking.

If I were one of those creatures, where would I be . . . ? Caruso slowed down. He thought . . . a place with decent road access. Not a main road per se . . . a decent secondary road, with a turn off to something more private. Easy in, easy out. A place where the neighbors couldn't see or hear what he's up to . . .

He picked up his microphone.

"Caruso to Birmingham Base."

"Yeah, Dominic," responded the agent on the radio desk. The FBI radios were encrypted, and couldn't be listened into by anyone without a good descrambler.

"The white van. How solid is that?"

"An elderly woman says that when she was out getting her paper, she saw a little girl, right description, talking to some guy next to a white van. The possible subject is male Caucasian, undetermined age, no other description. Ain't much, Dom, but it's all we got," Special Agent Sandy Ellis reported.

"How many child abusers in the area?" Caruso asked next.

"A total of nineteen on the computer. We got people talking to all of them. Nothing developed yet. All we got, man."

"Roger, Sandy. Out."

More driving, more scanning. He wondered if this was anything like his brother Brian had experienced in Afghanistan: alone, hunting the enemy . . . He started looking for dirt paths off the road, maybe for one with recent tire tracks.

He looked down at the wallet-sized photo again. A sweet-faced little girl, just learning the ABC's. A child for whom the world has always been a safe place, ruled by Mommy and Daddy, who went to Sunday school and made caterpillars out of egg cartons and pipe cleaners, and learned to sing "Jesus loves me, this I know / 'Cause the Bible tells me so . . ." His head swiveled left and right. There, about a hundred yards away, a dirt road leading into the woods. As he slowed, he saw that the path took a gentle S-curve, but the trees were thin, and he could see . . .

. . . cheap frame house . . . and next to it . . . the corner of a van . . . ? But this one was more beige than white . . .

Well, the little old lady who'd seen the little girl and the truck . . . how far away had it been . . . sunlight or shadows . . . ? So many things, so many inconstants, so many variables. As good as the FBI Academy was, it couldn't prepare you for everything—hell, not even close to everything. That's what they told you, too—told you that you had to trust your instinct and experience . . .

But Caruso had hardly a year's experience.

Still . . .

He stopped the car.

"Caruso to Birmingham Base."

"Yeah, Dominic," Sandy Ellis responded.

Caruso radioed in his location. "I'm going 10-7 to walk in and take a look."

"Roger that, Dom. Do you request backup?"

"Negative, Sandy. It's probably nothing, just going to knock on the door and talk to the occupant."

"Okay, I'll stand by."

Caruso didn't have a portable radio—that was for local cops, not the Bureau—and so was now out of touch, except for his cell phone. His personal side arm was a Smith & Wesson 1076, snug in its holster on his right hip. He stepped out of the car, and closed the door without latching it, to avoid making noise. People always turned to see what made the noise of a slammed car door.

He was wearing a darker than olive green suit, a fortunate circumstance, Caruso thought, heading right. First he'd look at the van. He walked normally, but his eyes were locked on the windows of the shabby house, halfway hoping to see a face, but, on reflection, glad that none appeared.

The Ford van was about six years old, he judged. Minor dings and dents on the bodywork. The driver had backed it in. That put the sliding door close to the house, the sort of thing a carpenter or plumber might do. Or a man moving a small, resisting body. He kept his right hand free, and his coat unbuttoned. Quick-draw was something every cop in the world practiced, often in front of a mirror, though only a fool fired as part of the motion, because you just couldn't hit anything that way.

Caruso took his time. The window was down on the driver-side door. The interior was almost entirely empty, bare, unpainted metal floor, the spare tire and jack . . . and a large roll of duct tape . . .

There was a lot of that stuff around. The free end of the roll was turned down, as though to make sure he'd be able to pull some off the roll without having to pick at it with his fingernails. A lot of people did that, too. There was, finally, a throw rug, tucked—no, *taped,* he saw, to the floor, just behind the right-side passenger seat . . . and was that some tape dangling from the metal seat framing? What might that mean?

Why there? Caruso wondered, but suddenly the skin on his forearms started tingling. It was a first for that sensation. He'd never made an arrest himself, had not yet been involved in a major felony case, at least not to any sort of conclusion. He'd worked fugitives in Newark, briefly, and made a total of three collars, always with another, more experienced agent to take the lead. He was more experienced now, a tiny bit seasoned . . . But not all that much, he reminded himself.

Caruso's head turned to the house. His mind was moving quickly now. What did he really have? Not much. He'd looked into an ordinary light truck with no direct evidence at all in it, just an empty truck with a roll of duct tape and a small rug on the steel floor.

Even so . . .

The young agent took the cell phone out of his pocket and speed-dialed the office.

"FBI. Can I help you?" a female voice asked.

"Caruso for Ellis." That moved things quickly.

"What you got, Dom?"

"White Ford Econoline van, Alabama tag Echo Romeo Six Five Zero One, parked at my location. Sandy—"

"Yeah, Dominic?"

"I'm going to knock on this guy's door."

"You want backup?"

Caruso took a second to think. "Affirmative—roger that."

"There's a county mountie about ten minutes away. Stand by," Ellis advised.

"Roger, standing by."

But a little girl's life was on the line . . .

He headed toward the house, careful to keep out of the sight lines from the nearest windows. That's when time stopped.

He nearly jumped out of his skin when he heard the scream. It was an awful, shrill sound, like someone looking at Death himself. His brain processed the information, and he suddenly found that his automatic pistol was in his hands, just in front of his sternum, pointed up into the sky, but in his hands even so. It had been a woman's scream, he realized, and something just went *click* inside his head.

As quickly as he could move without making much noise, he was on the porch, under the uneven, cheaply made roof. The front door was mostly wire screening to keep the bugs out. It needed painting, but so did the whole house. Probably a rental, and a cheap one at that. Looking through the screen he could see what seemed to be a corridor, leading left to the kitchen and right to a bathroom. He could see into it. A white porcelain toilet and a sink were all that was visible from this perspective.

He wondered if he had probable cause to enter the house, and instantly decided that he had enough. He pulled the door open and slipped in as stealthily as he could manage. A cheap and dirty rug leading down the corridor. He headed that way, gun up, senses sandpapered to ultimate alertness. As he moved, the angles of vision changed. The kitchen became invisible, but he could see into the bathroom better . . .

Penny Davidson was in the bathtub, naked, china blue eyes wide open, and her throat cut from ear to ear, with a whole body's supply of blood covering her flat chest and the sides of the tub. So violently had her neck been slashed that it lay open like a second mouth.

Strangely, Caruso didn't react physically. His eyes recorded the snapshot image, but for the moment all he thought about was that the man who'd done it was alive, and just a few feet away.

He realized that the noise he heard came from the left and ahead. The living room. A television. The subject would be in there. Might there be a second one? He didn't have time for that, nor did he particularly care at the moment.

Slowly, carefully, his heart going like a trip-hammer, he edged forward and peeked around the corner. There he was, late thirties, white male, hair thinning, watching the TV with rapt attention—it was a horror movie, the scream must have come from that—and sipping Miller Lite beer from an aluminum can. His face was content and in no way aroused. He'd probably been through that, Dominic thought. And right in front of him—Jesus—was a butcher knife, a bloody one, on the coffee table. There was blood on his T-shirt, as if sprayed. From a little girl's throat.

"The trouble with these mutts is that they never resist," an instructor had told his class at the FBI Academy. "Oh, yeah, they're John Wayne with an attitude when they have little kids in their hands, but they don't resist armed cops—ever. And, you know, that's a damned shame," the instructor had concluded.

You are not going in to jail today. The thought entered Caruso's mind seemingly of its own accord. His right thumb pulled back the spurless hammer until it clicked in place, putting his side arm fully in battery. His hands, he noted briefly, felt like ice.

Just at the corner, where you turned left to enter the room, was a battered old end table. Octagonal in shape, atop it was a transparent blue glass vase, a cheap one, maybe from the local Kmart, probably intended for flowers, but none were there today. Slowly, carefully, Caruso cocked his leg, then kicked the table over. The glass vase shattered loudly on the wooden floor.

The subject started violently, and turned to see an unexpected visitor in his house. His defensive response was instinctive rather than reasoned—he grabbed for the butcher knife on the coffee table. Caruso didn't even have time to smile, though he knew the subject had made the final mistake of his life. It's regarded as holy gospel in American police agencies that a man with a knife in his hand less than twenty-one feet away is an immediate and lethal threat. He even started to rise to his feet.

But he never made it.

Caruso's finger depressed the trigger of his Smith, sending the first round straight through the subject's heart. Two more followed in less than a second. His white T-shirt blossomed in red. He looked down at his chest, then up at Caruso, total surprise on his face, and then he sat back down, without speaking a word or crying out in pain.

Caruso's next action was to reverse direction and check out the house's only bedroom. Empty. So was the kitchen, the rear door still locked from the inside. There came a moment's relief. Nobody else in the house. He took another look at the kidnapper. The eyes were still open. But Dominic had shot true. First he disarmed and handcuffed the dead body, because that was how he'd been trained. A check of the carotid pulse came next, but it was wasted energy. The guy saw nothing except the front door of hell. Caruso pulled his cell phone out and speed-dialed the office again.

"Dom?" Ellis asked when he got the phone.

"Yeah, Sandy, it's me. I just took him down."

"What? What do you mean?" Sandy Ellis asked urgently.

"The little girl, she's here, dead, throat cut. I came in, and the guy came up at me with a knife. Took him down, man. He's dead, too, dead as fuckin' hell."

"Jesus, Dominic! The county sheriff is just a couple of minutes out. Stand by."

"Roger, standing by, Sandy."

Not another minute passed before he heard the sound of a siren. Caruso went out on the porch. He decocked and holstered his automatic, then he took his FBI credentials out of his coat pocket, and held them up in his left hand as the sheriff approached, his service revolver out.

"It's under control," Caruso announced in as calm a voice as he could muster. He was pumped up now. He waved Sheriff Turner into the house, but stayed outside by himself while the local cop went inside. A minute or two later, the cop came back out, his own Smith & Wesson holstered.

Turner was the Hollywood image of a southern sheriff, tall, heavyset, with beefy arms, and a gun belt that dug deeply into his waistline. Except he was black. Wrong movie.

"What happened?" he asked.

"Want to give me a minute?" Caruso took a deep breath and thought for a moment how to tell the story. Turner's understanding of it was important, because homicide was a local crime, and he had jurisdiction over it.

"Yeah." Turner reached into his shirt pocket and pulled out a pack of Kools. He offered one to Caruso, who shook his head.

The young agent sat down on the unpainted wooden deck and tried to put it all together in his head. What, exactly, had happened? What, exactly, had he just done? And how, exactly, was he supposed to explain it? The whispering part of his mind told him that he felt no regret at all. At least not for the subject. For Penelope Davidson—too damned late. An hour sooner? Maybe even a half hour? That little girl would not be going home tonight, would never more be tucked into bed by her mother, or hug her father. And so Special Agent Dominic Caruso felt no remorse at all. Just regret for being too slow.

"Can you talk?" Sheriff Turner asked.

"I was looking for a place like this one, and when I drove past, I saw the van parked . . ." Caruso began. Presently, he stood and led the sheriff into the house to relate the other details.

"Anyway, I tripped over the table. He saw me, and went for his knife, turned toward me—and so, I drew my pistol and shot the bastard. Three rounds, I think."

"Uh-huh." Turner went over to the body. The subject hadn't bled much. All three rounds had gone straight through the heart, ending its ability to pump almost instantly.

Paul Turner wasn't anywhere nearly as dumb as he looked to a government-trained agent. He looked at the body, and turned to look back at the doorway from which Caruso had taken his shots. His eyes measured distance and angle.

"So," the sheriff said, "you tripped on that end table. The suspect sees you, grabs his knife, and you, being in fear of your life, take out your service pistol and take three quick shots, right?"

"That's how it went down, yeah."

"Uh-huh," observed a man who got himself a deer almost every hunting season.

Sheriff Turner reached into his right-side pants pocket and pulled out his key chain. It was a gift from his father, a Pullman porter on the old Illinois Central. It was an old-fashioned one, with a 1948 silver dollar soldered onto it, the old kind, about an inch and a half across. He held it over the kidnapper's chest, and the diameter of the old coin completely covered all three of the entrance wounds. His eyes took a very skeptical look, but then they drifted over toward the bathroom, and his eyes softened before he spoke his verdict on the incident.

"Then that's how we'll write it up. Nice shootin', boy."

FULLY A dozen police and FBI vehicles appeared within as many minutes. Soon thereafter came the lab truck from the Alabama Department of Public Safety to perform the crime-scene investigative work. A forensic photographer shot twenty-three rolls of 400-speed color film. The knife was taken from the subject's hand and bagged for fingerprints and blood-type matching with the victim—it was all less than a formality, but criminal procedure was especially strict in a murder case. Finally, the body of the little girl was bagged and removed. Her parents would have to identify her, but blessedly her face was reasonably intact.

One of the last to arrive was Ben Harding, the Special Agent in Charge of the Birmingham Field Office of the Federal Bureau of Investigation. An agent-involved shooting meant a formal report from his desk to that of Director Dan Murray, a distant friend. First, Harding came to make sure that Caruso was in decent physical and psychological shape. Then he went to pay respects to Paul Turner, and get his opinion of the shooting. Caruso watched from a distance, and saw Turner gesture through the incident, accompanied by nods from Harding. It was good that Sheriff Turner was giving his official stamp of approval. A captain of state troopers listened in as well, and he nodded, too.

The truth of the matter was that Dominic Caruso didn't really give a damn. He knew he'd done the right thing, just an hour later than it ought to have been. Finally, Harding came over to his young agent.

"How you feeling, Dominic?"

"Slow," Caruso said. "Too damned slow—yeah, I know, unreasonable to expect otherwise."

Harding grabbed his shoulder and shook it. "You could not have done much better, kid." He paused. "How'd the shooting go down?"

Caruso repeated his story. It had almost acquired the firmness of truth in his mind now. He could probably have spoken the exact truth and not been hammered for it, Dom knew, but why take the chance? It was, officially, a clean shoot, and that was enough, so far as his Bureau file was concerned.

Harding listened, and nodded thoughtfully. There'd be paperwork to complete and FedEx up the line to D.C. But it would not look bad in the newspapers for an FBI agent to have shot and killed a kidnapper the very day of the crime. They'd probably find evidence that this was not the only such crime this mutt had committed. The house had yet to be thoroughly searched. They'd already found a digital camera in the house, and it would surprise no one to see that the mutt had a record of previous crimes on his Dell personal computer. If so, Caruso had closed more than one case. If so, Caruso would get a big gold star in his Bureau copybook.

Just how big, neither Harding nor Caruso could yet know. The talent hunt was about to find Dominic Caruso, too.

And one other.

CHAPTER 1

THE
CAMPUS

THE TOWN of West Odenton, Maryland, isn't much of a town at all, just a post office for people who live in the general area, a few gas stations and a 7-Eleven, plus the usual fast-food places for people who need a fat-filled breakfast on the drive from Columbia, Maryland, to their jobs in Washington, D.C. And half a mile from the modest post office building was a mid-rise office building of government-undistinguished architecture. It was nine stories high, and on the capacious front lawn a low decorative monolith made of gray brick with silvery lettering said HENDLEY ASSOCIATES, without explaining what, exactly, Hendley Associates was. There were few hints. The roof of the building was flat, tar-and-gravel over reinforced concrete, with a small penthouse to house the elevator machinery and another rectangular structure that gave no clue about its identity. In fact, it was made of fiberglass, white in color, and radio-transparent. The building itself was unusual only in one thing: except for a few old tobacco barns that barely exceeded twenty-five feet in height, it was the only building higher than two stories that sat on a direct line of sight from the National Security Agency located at Fort Meade, Maryland, and the headquarters of the Central Intelligence Agency at Langley, Virginia. Some other entrepreneurs had wished to build on that sight line, but zoning approval had never been granted, for many reasons, all of them false.

Behind the building was a small antenna farm not unlike that found next to a local television station—a half-dozen six-meter parabolic dishes sat inside a twelve-foot-high, razor-wire-crowned Cyclone fence enclosure and pointed at various commercial communications satellites. The entire complex, which wasn't terribly complex at all, comprised fifteen and a third acres in Maryland's Howard County, and was referred to as "The Campus" by the people who worked there. Nearby was the Johns Hopkins University Applied Physics Laboratory, a government-consulting establishment of long standing and well-established sensitivity of function.

To the public, Hendley Associates was a trader in stocks, bonds, and international currencies, though, oddly, it did little in the way of public business. It was not known to have any clients, and while it was whispered to be quietly active in local charities (the Johns Hopkins University School of Medicine was rumored to be the main recipient of Hendley's corporate largesse), nothing had ever leaked to the local media. In fact, it had no public-relations department at all. Neither was it rumored to be doing anything untoward, though its chief executive officer was known to have had a somewhat troubled past, as a result of which he was shy of publicity, which, on a few rare occasions, he'd dodged quite adroitly and amiably, until, finally, the local media had stopped asking. Hendley's employees were scattered about locally, mostly in Columbia, lived an upper-middle-class lifestyle, and were generally as remarkable as Beaver's father, Ward Cleaver.

Gerald Paul Hendley, Jr., had had a stellar career in the commodities business, during which he'd amassed a sizable personal fortune and then turned to elected public service in his late thirties, soon becoming a United States senator from South Carolina. Very quickly, he'd acquired a reputation as a legislative maverick who eschewed special interests and their campaign money offers, and followed a rather ferociously independent political track, leaning toward liberal on civil-rights issues, but decidedly conservative on defense and foreign relations. He'd never shied away from speaking his mind, which had made him good and entertain-